Terror
in the
High Sierras

Bob Wright

D1457259

A **PERSPECTIVES** BOOK
High Noon Books
Novato, California

Series Editor: Penn Mullin
Cover and Illustrations: Herb Heidinger

International Standard Book Number: 0-87879-300-3

9 8 7 6
20 19 18 17 16 15 14

You'll enjoy all the High Noon Books. Write for
a free complete list of titles.

Contents

Chapter 1

Bigfoot is Back

Greg slid out from under his red '67 Chevy pickup. Spots of oil were all over his shirt and pants. "You said what?"

"I said the newspaper says that Bigfoot has been spotted. This time he was seen in the Sierras," Kirk called back.

"Big what? Wait a minute. Let me turn off the engine. I can't hear what you're talking about," yelled Greg.

Kirk was standing by the garage door. He was reading the newspaper. Greg shut off the engine. It was quiet now.

"Bigfoot. Bigfoot. You know. That animal or monster or thing. It has been seen in the mountains again this summer. It's scaring everyone out of the mountains. Some people are missing. They think they may have been killed by this thing," Kirk answered.

1

"So what's it got to do with us?" Greg asked.

"Well, why not go to the Sierras? We could camp there instead of at Yellowstone. Maybe we'll see it," Kirk said.

Greg and Kirk had been planning a camping trip. They were going to go to Yellowstone. Greg started to wipe off his tools and clean his hands. He was thinking. It was OK with him. The pickup was all ready to make the trip.

"The Sierras are closer to get to than Yellowstone. So that isn't a problem. Are you sure you want to look for something that dangerous?" asked Greg.

"Sure I'm sure. Look at this newspaper. Bigfoot has been seen only a few times. There are just a few fuzzy pictures of him. No one has really gotten a good look. We might get a good picture of him. We could sell it to the newspapers," Kirk answered.

"Man, you're going too fast. What else do you know about Bigfoot?" Greg asked.

"Well," said Kirk, "it says here that Indians knew of him. He has been called Yehti and Sasquatch. They think he is about ten feet tall. He walks on two feet like a bear or an ape. He probably weighs about 300 pounds. No one knows what he eats. They think he might be a meat-eater."

"He sounds dangerous to me," added Greg, "but I can bring my rifle."

Everything was quiet again. Greg was thinking.

"Well, I have a camera. You have a rifle. Are you game to give it a try?" Kirk asked.

"Sure, I'm sure. Look at this newspaper."

"Sure, why not? Live it up, I say."

Greg took Kirk's newspaper. He looked at the drawing of Bigfoot. The newspaper said that people were being asked not to go near Peak's Valley in the Sierras. That is where Bigfoot had been spotted.

"I know one thing for sure, the pickup is ready," Greg said. "It may look like a clunker but it has guts. It can handle those mountain roads. Will you be ready in the morning?"

"Be by at seven. I'll load my things on the truck then," Kirk answered.

"Don't forget the road map. I don't know that area too well," said Greg.

"Don't worry," Kirk called back. "I know how to get there."

Greg still had the newspaper. He looked at the picture of Bigfoot. What if they did see him? What would they do? He got his 30-30 and wrapped it. He put it in the back of the pickup. That was one thing for sure he wanted to have with him.

Chapter 2

Heading for Sawdust

At seven o'clock sharp, Greg was in front of Kirk's house. He honked his horn three times.

"OK, OK, you're waking up everyone. Cool it. I'll be right there," Kirk called.

Greg already had his gear on the pickup. Kirk came out with things they needed for the one-week trip. He had a small tent, his sleeping bag, cooking supplies, a lantern, a fishing rod, a flashlight, and other things. He tossed them onto the pickup. Then he jumped into the front seat and said, "OK, let's go."

Greg looked at him. "Did you bring a camera to take any pictures of Bigfoot? That is, in case we see him?"

"Not only my Polaroid, but plenty of film."

"How about the map?"

"Right here. Just follow route 73 up to Greyton. Then hook into Highway 109. We can stop at Sawdust to get directions to Peak's Valley. Do you have your rifle?"

"I sure do. It's right here." Greg pointed to the space in back of the seat. It was there, all wrapped up.

All the way to Sawdust, Kirk was talking. He wanted to get some good pictures of Bigfoot. He kept telling Kirk how much money he would make from the pictures.

It took about six hours to get to Sawdust. It had once been a big town. The goldminers used to pan and dig for gold there. That was about a hundred years ago. There had been a big mine called The Three Aces. It held millions of dollars in gold. No one knew its location now. The town dropped from 40,000 to a few hundred in just two years. Sawdust now had a bank, a general store, a handful of houses, a gas station, a restaurant, and a sheriff's office. Many people on their way to the mountains stopped at Sawdust before going on.

Greg pulled into the gas station.

"What will it be?" said a young lady in jeans.

"Fill it up," answered Greg, "with regular."

"I wonder if she just works here or owns the station," Kirk said.

The girl had heard Kirk speaking. "My father

owns it. I just work here part time," she said.

She finished pumping the gas. Then she said, "I'll check under the hood for you."

Greg jumped out of the pickup. "No, that's OK. I'll do it myself." He checked the oil and tightened the screw on the carburetor.

"Having trouble with the carburetor?" she asked.

"I did an adjustment on it last week. It think it still needs some work," Greg answered.

"Well," she said, "if you need a rebuilt one, let me know. My dad or I can fix it. You guys going into the hills to look for Bigfoot?"

By this time Kirk was out of the truck. "We sure are," he said.

"Well, I just like to camp and fish. Kirk wants to look for Bigfoot," Greg said.

"Be careful. People have been hurt looking for him. Last week two people were killed. They fell off the side of the mountain. Yesterday another man came out of the mountains. He was all beat up. A lot of campers have been leaving."

"Has Bigfoot been seen in just one area?" Kirk asked.

"People say it has been in the area where The Three Aces mine is supposed to be," she said. "A lot of people still think they might find that

7

mine. My dad says it still has gold in it."

"By the way, what's your name? And what do we owe you for the gas?" Greg asked.

"$16.50 and my name is Jeanie. You have a full tank now," she said.

Greg gave her a twenty dollar bill. "Any other ideas for keeping safe while we're up here?"

"Just stay clear of places with lots of trees. Stay away from rocky places. Bigfoot seems to come out of nowhere," Jeanie said. She gave Greg his change.

"What's the best way to get into Peak's Valley?" Greg asked.

"Follow the highway north for about another fifteen miles. You'll see an old white house with a lot of pine trees around it. Take the dirt road to the right of it. Follow that road for another fifteen miles. Then you'll be in the Valley. I'll draw a map for you," Jeanie said. She gave Greg the map.

"I'm hungry," Kirk said. "How's the restaurant?"

"It's the only one in town. You don't have much of a choice. But they do have a good meal," she said. "Just one last tip. Try to get into the Valley before it gets dark. It's bad enough during the day. The road is really bad."

"Take the dirt road to the right of the white house, 'til you reach the valley."

Greg and Kirk both got back into the pickup.

Greg yelled out, "Thanks for your help."

"That's OK," Jeanie called. "Drop by on your way back from camping."

They drove the pickup down to the restaurant. They got a good meal and were on their way by four o'clock.

Chapter 3

Old Trails Have Surprises

Greg was thinking about getting into the Valley before dark. He kept his foot on the gas pedal. He and Kirk were both thinking about what Jeanie had said. The newspaper hadn't told about so many people being hurt.

"Jeanie was a lot of help," said Kirk.

"She sure was and cute, too," replied Greg. "That story about the lost gold mine is something."

"Well, maybe we'll find both," Kirk said.

"Fat chance," Greg answered.

Suddenly Kirk yelled. "There it is. That's the old house Jeanie told us about."

Greg took a right turn off the highway. The dirt road was bumpy. "Jeanie wasn't kidding when she said to get here before dark. This is one road we can't go fast on," he said.

The road was like an old trail. The pickup was

bouncing from one side to the other. The sun was beginning to set. They still hadn't reached the Valley. Kirk turned his portable radio on. All he could get was static. "It won't work through the trees," he said.

They both remembered what Jeanie had said about trees. Greg had to stop two times to clear branches that were in the way. It was starting to get dark. By this time he had to turn his headlights on. They both had to watch carefully. Greg drove slowly.

Kirk suddenly sat up straight. "Stop the truck!" he yelled.

Greg stopped quickly. "What's the matter?"

"Look ahead. I see two things shining at us. They're like eyes," said Kirk.

Greg saw them. Sure enough, there were two big balls flashing at them.

"It's Bigfoot!" Kirk screamed. The eyes seemed to move toward them. Then he said, "It's only a horse!"

By this time the lights of the pickup were right on it. "It's a mule," said Greg. "Look at the ears."

A mule, with a sidebag, was standing off the side of the road. It was staring at the pickup, blinking its eyes.

"Who in the world would be using a mule these days?" asked Kirk.

"Look there, by the mule. Come on. There's a man lying there," Greg said.

They both jumped out of the pickup. An old man was lying by the side of the road. He was all beat up.

"Good grief! Bigfoot has been here."

"Good grief! Bigfoot has been here. He's killed this man."

Kirk was ready to make Greg turn the pickup around and go back home.

"We can't leave him here," Greg said. "He may be alive. Get your flashlight. Bring the canteen too."

Kirk ran back to the pickup. He kept thinking that Bigfoot might be hiding near the trees. Maybe the same thing might happen to him and Greg.

"Hurry up," Greg called. "Where's the flashlight?"

Kirk came running back with the flashlight and the canteen. Greg bent over the man.

"He's breathing," Greg said. "He's alive, but he's been hurt." The man had long white hair and a white beard. His clothes were old. He had marks on his head. His shirt was torn. Greg raised his head. They didn't want to move him. They gave him a little water. The man groaned. He opened his eyes and said, "Where's Lady?" Then he closed his eyes.

"I think he might be OK. We won't move him," Greg said.

"Did he say a lady hit him?" Kirk asked.

"He said something," Greg replied. "Let's

pitch the tent here. It's off the road. I'll leave the pickup there. No one will use this road at night. We'll be safe until morning."

Greg got the tent from the bed of the pickup. They put it up over the old man. Then they put a blanket over him. Kirk decided to sleep in the pickup. Greg slept by the tent. They would wait until morning before moving the man.

Chapter 4

Rufus Talks

It was cold the next morning. Greg and Kirk woke early. They heard the old man moving. He seemed to be talking to himself. He seemed to be trying to get up. They both got dressed quickly. Greg got to the tent first.

"Where am I? What happened? Where's Lady?" the old man asked.

"Don't worry. You're OK," Greg said. The old man was trying to sit up in the tent. "Looks like you got roughed up last night, old man."

"Don't call me old man. My name is Rufus, Rufus Jennings. Help me get out of here. And where's Lady?" Rufus asked.

"Who's Lady?" Greg asked.

"She's my friend," Rufus said.

"Kirk," Greg called, "start a fire. Put some coffee on."

"Now you're talking," Rufus said. Greg

grabbed Rufus's hand. He helped him get out of the tent. All Rufus could say was "Ow, oh, oh, ow!"

When he was out he tried to stand up. Greg helped him. Then Rufus said, "There you are, Lady. You OK?" He was talking to the mule.

Kirk had gotten some small twigs and branches. He cleared a spot for the fire. Then he put the coffee pot over it on a grill.

"You had better stay still for awhile. You might have a broken bone," Kirk said to Rufus.

"Broken bone, my foot," Rufus said. "I was hit on the head. I have one big headache. That's all! I was jumped on yesterday. I don't know who done it. But someone jumped me from behind. Didn't take anything. Lady is still loaded with my tools."

Rufus looked at Greg and Kirk. They wondered if Rufus thought they had jumped him last night. Greg said, "We didn't do it. We saw you lying by the road. We put the tent over you."

"Greg, come here, quick!" Kirk called. He had gone over to the truck.

All around one side of the truck there were large footprints in the soft ground. Rufus walked slowly over to the truck. "Them ain't no animal prints," he said. "Too big for a bear, that's for sure." The footprints were about a foot long and about eight inches wide, with five big toes.

"Is anything missing?" Kirk asked.

Greg checked the supplies. Then he yelled, "My rifle is gone!" Sure enough, it was not in the back of the seat.

"This is nuts," Greg said. "Rufus gets beat up.

All around one side of the truck there were large footprints.

Nothing is taken from him. Then we find these prints just around the truck. And the only thing missing is my rifle!" Greg was mad. "I don't like any of this."

By this time the coffee was ready. Kirk got the cups from the pickup. They all sat down.

"Do you live up here?" Greg asked Rufus.

"I don't tell other people this. But you both helped me. Maybe saved my life. I pan for gold. See the stream over there? The gold washes out from the old mines up in those hills. I used to find a lot there every spring. Then I'd take it to the bank in Sawdust. Last year I didn't find very much. One of these days I'm going to find The Three Aces mine. Then I'll be rich," Rufus said.

"What is The Three Aces mine?" Kirk asked.

"Well, sonny," Rufus said, "it was one of the biggest mines up here a hundred years ago. The three men who found it kept it secret. Then they all died of scarlet fever. No one has ever been able to find it. You aren't looking for it, are you?"

"No," Kirk said, "we're looking for Bigfoot. Maybe we're close." He looked back at the big footprints by the pickup.

"Maybe we're closer than we think," Greg said.

"I can't figure this out," Rufus said. "I get

banged up. Then you guys find strange tracks around your truck. Only your rifle is missing. A wild animal would have jumped on the truck. It would have taken food, not the rifle. There was never anything like a Bigfoot here in these parts before. And I'm not getting as much gold as usual this year. Sure is strange."

"I'm hungry," Kirk said.

"Does that stream have trout?" Greg asked.

"Sure does. Nice ones," Rufus answered.

Greg got up to get his pole from the pickup.

Suddenly Lady started making noises. A camper drove up. It stopped by Greg's pickup.

A man and a woman got out.

"I smell trouble," Rufus said.

Chapter 5

Mysterious Visitors

The man and woman walked up to the fire.

"Hello. I'm Jim Wall, and this is my wife, Betty. We've been camping down the road. We're near the stream, too."

"I'm Greg. This is Kirk and this is Rufus Jennings. Can we be of any help?" Greg said.

"Well, we're not sure. We've been camping upstream for a week. Last night we heard sounds around our camper. Then we heard banging on the camper door. This morning we found that the door was all smashed up. We found big footprints around the camper. Everything we left outside was all torn up. We heard about Bigfoot being around here. We're scared. We're going to leave. How about all of you?" Jim said.

They looked at the camper door. It was all banged up.

"Do you think it was Bigfoot?" Kirk asked.

"We sure do," Jim said.

"We didn't hear anything last night. But we found footprints this morning around our pickup. Nothing was banged up, but my rifle is missing," Greg said.

"And I was beat up yesterday," Rufus said.

"Did you see anything?" Betty asked.

"No, just the tracks," Greg answered.

"I think we all had better be careful. Our radio said that two more people have been found dead. And two others are in Sawdust. They are very badly beaten up," said Betty.

"Heck! I want to get a picture of Bigfoot," Kirk said.

"I wouldn't try anything like that. This thing is dangerous. It could tear you to pieces," Jim said. "We saw you pull in last night. We just wanted to let you know we are leaving. You're the only ones left around here now. If something else happened, it would be hard to get any help."

Betty said, "I just want to get out of here. I'm scared!"

"Maybe we will leave, too," Greg said. "But we want to make sure that Rufus is OK before we do anything."

"Old timer," Jim said, "you might want to move on to other parts. It's too dangerous here to be panning for gold."

Rufus didn't like the "old timer" that Jim used. He didn't say anything.

Jim and Betty went back to the camper. "We're leaving. We hope you will, too," Betty called out. They turned the camper around and went back down the road.

"I don't like them folks. I just don't like them," Rufus said.

"Oh, they're OK," Kirk said.

"Nope! I been all over this place. I sure didn't see them by the stream where they said they was. They was nowhere near it. And the dent in their camper door wasn't made by any animal!" Rufus said.

"Well, for now, I feel like some fresh trout," Greg said. "Why don't you stay here with Rufus, Kirk? I'll see what I can get." He got his pole and said to Rufus, "Any good places on the stream?"

"Yeah. Go upstream a little. You'll find a pool. It isn't deep. The fish like it," Rufus replied.

Greg got his pole. He went over to the stream. He walked along it. He found the pool. Everything was quiet. As he cast he heard some noises in back of him. He turned around. Through the woods he saw the camper. It was under some trees. He figured the Walls stopped to get a few things. Then he turned around to see what he could catch. The stream was full of trout. It didn't take long to get three. He turned around to start back to Kirk and Rufus. The camper was still there. Greg decided to go over to it. Maybe Bigfoot had come around during the day. Maybe something had happened.

As he got near the camper, he heard voices. He knew it wasn't a radio. At first he thought it was just Jim and Betty. Then he heard other voices. The Walls had said they were alone. But Greg could hear the voices of other men. Then he heard laughing. Then talking again. The Walls had said there were no other people in the Valley. Greg went back to the stream. He walked back the same way to Kirk and Rufus.

Kirk saw Greg coming with the fish. "I'll get the pan ready," he called.

Greg was quiet. Then he said, "Something is fishy, here. And it isn't just the fish!"

"What do you mean?" Kirk asked.

"It's the Walls, isn't it?" Rufus said.

"Sure is," Greg said. He told them about seeing the camper. And he told them about hearing other voices.

"I don't like this at all," Rufus said. "Mighty

strange."

Kirk started to clean the fish. Rufus was watching him. "Here. Let me do that," Rufus said. "You're making a mess out of them, lad."

After breakfast they sat and talked for awhile. Why did the Walls say everyone had left the Valley except them? Why did they stop when they said they were leaving? All Rufus could say was, "I knew them people meant trouble."

In the afternoon Rufus was feeling better. He showed Greg and Kirk the high cliffs. They could see caves up there. There were many mines here a hundred years ago. One of them might be The Three Aces.

That night after supper they decided to stay one more day. Rufus said he might pan in the next valley. Rufus had his own tent. He put it up. Greg and Kirk used their own. They were all settled and it was quiet.

Then, suddenly, they heard a terrible screaming sound.

Chapter 6

Bigfoot Strikes!

It woke the three of them. The noise was terrible. There was screaming and yelling. Then it stopped. It was dark. It was quiet. Greg reached for his flashlight, but it wasn't there.

Something suddenly grabbed Kirk's foot. He screamed.

"Shhhhh," Rufus said. "It's me." Rufus had crawled from his tent over to Greg and Kirk. "Something is out there. It ain't no animal."

Lady was making noises. Greg, Kirk, and Rufus were waiting to see what would happen. They heard sounds like big steps coming toward the tent. Then something like a huge claw started to rip the tent. The three of them were frozen with fear. Greg found his flashlight. He shined it through a hole in the tent. They all saw a huge animal standing there. It didn't do anything.

"Kirk, run and get the rifle," Greg yelled.

Kirk got out of the tent. He ran for the pickup, tripped, got up, and stopped. "It was stolen, remember?" he called out.

Then the big animal started growling and screaming and running around. It was huge. It looked just like they thought it would. It was big and hairy. Then, just as quickly as it had come, it ran off into the trees. The night was quiet again.

Kirk found his camera. "Come on," he called. "Let's chase it. I want to get a picture of it."

"Are you crazy?" Greg yelled. "Let it alone!"

The three of them decided to sleep in the pickup.

"This whole thing is nuts," said Rufus. "I never had this happen before. I been here thirty-seven years. No animal ever did that!"

They had blankets with them. They were soon all asleep. In the morning Rufus woke up first. He got out to check on Lady. She was fine. He let her loose to feed on the grass. By this time Greg and Kirk were up. Kirk was starting the fire.

Greg was trying to check on tracks that might be around. He followed them to the trees. Then they just stopped.

"This doesn't make any sense," Greg said. "It's just like yesterday. The tracks just stop. They don't go anywhere."

"Do you think it can swing in the trees like an ape?" Kirk asked.

"Kirk, apes use heavy vines. There aren't any vines in these trees," Greg said.

The tent was a mess. It was all clawed up.

"If I just had my rifle," Greg said. "We could have stopped that thing."

"And my camera. If I just could have gotten a picture of it," Kirk added.

"Maybe we should have left yesterday," Greg said.

Kirk almost had the coffee ready. They all had a cup of it.

"I don't like them Walls," said Rufus, "but maybe we should see if they heard anything last night."

"Good idea," said Greg. "Let's all go over there. Maybe they are still there."

They went the same way as Greg had gone the day before. They went along the stream to the pool. The camper wasn't there.

"Well," Kirk said, "we were wrong. They did leave."

"I want to go over to where their camper was," Greg said.

"Good idea," Rufus said. "We just might find

something over there."

When they got there, they didn't find anything. Greg could see fresh tire tracks left in the grass. They didn't go back to the road. That was strange, he thought.

"I can't figure this out," Greg said. "The camper is gone, but the tracks don't go to the road."

"I think we should follow the fresh tire tracks," Rufus said. "We might find something."

They walked slowly through the short grass. Then Kirk said, "I see it. The camper is ahead. I see it in those trees."

Chapter 7

An Amazing Discovery

Sure enough, the camper was hidden in another grove of trees. There were branches all over it. Someone was trying to keep it hidden. Kirk, Greg, and Rufus walked slowly toward the camper. There were no noises coming from it. But was someone hiding inside?

"You guys stay here," Greg said. "Let me check it out."

Kirk and Rufus stayed behind. Greg went ahead by himself. He slowly walked up to the camper. He waited. Then he tried to open the door. The door was locked. He was able to look through one of the windows. What he saw surprised him. He went running back to Kirk and Rufus.

"They're not there," he said, "But they have picks, shovels, and other tools in the camper."

"I knew it," Rufus said. "I didn't like them people the first time I saw them!" Suddenly Rufus stopped. "Listen," he said, "I hear voices."

"I don't hear anything," Kirk said.

"Shh — listen. You will," Rufus said.

They all stood very quietly. Then they heard soft voices. They seemed to be a long way off. They also heard banging, but it was soft, too.

"I know these mountains," Rufus said. "You think a sound is coming from one place but it is coming from another. It can confuse you."

"I think the sounds are coming from over there," Kirk said.

"Nope! They're not," Rufus said. "They're coming from up on the cliffs. I think we better see what is going on."

"Rufus, what do you think is going on?" Greg asked.

"I don't like this. The gold gave out in the stream. We're attacked by something. We hear voices from those hills and cliffs. The Three Aces Mine is somewhere up there. You saw shovels and picks in the camper," Rufus said.

"Rufus," Greg said, "do you think someone found The Three Aces?"

Rufus didn't say anything for a minute. Then he said. "Yep—I sure do. And I want to find those critters. That's my mine! Let's go up there and get them!"

"Rufus," said Greg, "how are we going to get them? I don't even have my rifle. There could be many people up there. We wouldn't have a chance."

"Well, let's go see what they're doing," Rufus said.

"Wait," Kirk said, "let me get my camera. Just in case."

"OK," Greg said. "But hurry."

"While he's gone, we'll decide what to do," Rufus said.

"Rufus," Greg said, "I don't think you should go with us. You're still sore from the other night. Tell me the way. We'll go. Then we'll come back and tell you what we saw."

Rufus didn't like the idea. But he knew he was still sore. "OK," he said. "Down by the pool where you fished there is a small dry creek bed that washes down from the hills each spring. Follow that small creek bed. But be careful. Listen for voices as you get near the top. That's where I think they are."

Kirk came back with his camera. They walked back to the pool. Rufus showed them where the small path was. He said he would wait by the pool for them. The small path was behind some big boulders. They started to walk along it. It was so small, they couldn't walk together. Greg went first. They couldn't go fast. The path curved. In many places it was slippery.

After an hour they were still climbing. They were sure that only Rufus knew the path. They felt safe on it. They looked down to the meadow. It seemed a long way down. It was a steep climb.

"We seem to be getting closer," Kirk said. "The voices are louder."

"Remember what Rufus said about sounds. They seem to be one place, but they're coming from another," Greg said.

Suddenly Greg stopped. He grabbed onto Kirk. He whispered, "Stop. Don't move. Don't say anything. Just look over this rock. But be careful."

Kirk slowly looked over the top of the big rock. About 100 yards away they saw ten men. They had shovels and wheelbarrows. They were going in and out of a cave. Rufus had told them there were many caves in these hills.

They both sat behind the rock. What if someone could see them? "Greg, do you think this might be The Three Aces mine?" Kirk said.

"It could be," Greg said. "I think Rufus was

right about the Walls."

"Why?" asked Kirk.

"Take another look. But be careful," Greg whispered again.

Kirk looked over the top of the big rock again. He could see Jim and Betty. They were sitting outside a tent near the cave. He got back down.

"Rufus was right about them," Kirk said.

"Did you see anything else?" Greg asked.

"No," Kirk said, "just the men and the Walls. Isn't that enough?"

"Take one more look," Greg said.

Again Kirk looked over the big rock. He was very careful not to be seen. Suddenly he got down. "Where's my camera?" he asked.

"You saw it?" Greg said.

"I sure did," Kirk replied.

Both Greg and Kirk had seen the same thing. They had seen the men, the shovels, the cave, and the Walls. The other thing they saw was a big, hairy, flat thing hanging on the tent. Kirk took several shots of it with his Polaroid.

"Greg," Kirk said, "that's a costume. It's a Bigfoot costume!"

"That's right," Greg said. "Bigfoot is not Bigfoot. It looks like the Walls have been trying to scare us."

Kirk slowly looked over the top of the big rock.

"Let's get out of here," Kirk said.

"I'm with you," Greg said.

The two of them moved fast. They were quiet and careful. They almost ran down the creek bed back to Rufus.

Chapter 8

The Three Aces

Rufus was sleeping when Greg and Kirk got back to the stream. He woke up when they were at the pool. He could tell they had news.

"Well, what did you find?" he asked them. He knew they had plenty to tell.

Greg spoke first. "You were right about the Walls. They are up there. They have about ten men with them. They're working a mine."

"What do you mean working a mine?" Rufus asked.

"The men had wheelbarrows. They had picks and shovels. They were taking dirt out of the mine," Greg said.

"And," Kirk said, "Bigfoot is a costume!"

"What do you mean?" Rufus asked.

"He means that someone is putting on a costume to make it look like Bigfoot has been here!" Greg said.

Rufus sat quietly for a moment. He looked like he had been hit over the head again. Then he jumped up. "I knew it! I knew it!" he yelled. "It's The Three Aces. They found it. I've been looking for it for years. They found it. They found my mine!"

Greg and Kirk sat down. No wonder the Walls were trying to scare people. They were using Bigfoot to get people out of the Valley. That way they could work the mine without any trouble.

"This is a matter for the police," said Greg. "We better get back to Sawdust."

"But everyone will find out about my mine," Rufus said.

"Rufus, people have been hurt by these crooks. They are dangerous," Greg said.

Rufus tied Lady to a tree. He didn't want to leave her alone. But he was worried about the mine. He and Kirk and Greg went back to the pickup in a hurry. They all got in the front seat.

All the way to Sawdust, Rufus kept talking. He told them again how he had been looking for The Three Aces for years. He said it was *his* mine. It was *his* gold.

They stopped at the gas station in town.

"Hi, what's up, you guys? Hi, Rufus, how are you?" Jeanie called out.

"Hi, Jeanie," Greg said. "We need to get to the police station. Can you tell us which way to go?"

"I hope Rufus isn't in any trouble," she said.

"No, he isn't. Do you know Rufus?" Kirk asked.

"Oh, sure," she said. "Everyone here knows Rufus."

Greg said, "We think we've found out about Bigfoot."

"Wait," she said, "I want to go with you. Anyway, the police station will be easier to get to if I show you the way."

Kirk got out and got on the back of the pickup. Jeanie got in the front seat with Greg and Rufus. She called out, "Dad, I have to leave for awhile. I'll be back." She waved to her father.

"The police station is one more block. Then hang a left," she said.

Greg said, "Jeanie, you could have told us that."

"I know," she said, "but I wanted to find out what you know about Bigfoot and all the trouble up here. You know, it hasn't been good for Sawdust. People who camp in the mountains buy things here. And that means they also buy gas. When people don't come up here camping, we lose business."

They all went into the police station. "Hi,

They all went into the police station.

Jeanie, can I help you?" said an officer. Kirk was the first one to say anything.

"Sir," he said, "we think we've found out why there has been trouble at Peak's Valley."

Officer Burns stopped him. "Wait a minute. Are you talking about Bigfoot?"

"That's right," Greg said. "We think some

people found The Three Aces."

Now Rufus stopped them. "*My* mine, you mean!"

Officer Burns looked at Rufus. Then back at Greg. "Go on," he said.

"We think these people found The Three Aces. We think they have been scaring people away. This way they could work the mine without any trouble from other people," Greg said.

"Them Walls and their camper," Rufus said. "I smelled trouble when I first saw them."

Now Jeanie stopped everyone. "Wait a minute," she said. "Do they have a green camper?"

"Yes, it's green," Kirk said.

"I knew something was funny about those people. No one goes camping for eight weeks in those hills. And remember, Officer Burns, I told you two weeks ago they were buying a lot of food for just two people," Jeanie said.

"Yes, you did tell me that," Officer Burns said. "But, Jeanie, you can't stop people from buying food. And I can't get my men and go up there unless you can give me a reason. How do I know you're right?"

"Is this enough for you?" Kirk said. He took out the picures that showed Jim and Betty and the men.

Officer Burns looked at them. He said, "I think this is all we need."

He sent out a call for three police cars. He told his men to take their rifles.

"What about the mine?" Kirk asked.

"That mine is public property. No one can take it. If this whole story is true, those people are in big, big trouble," Officer Burns said.

Rufus got in a car with Officer Burns. The three police cars followed Greg, Kirk, and Jeanie back into Peak's Valley.

They all parked near the trees. "I'll stay here with Rufus," Jeanie said.

Greg and Kirk showed the police the way up to the top. When they got there, they all spread out. Officer Burns called out, "Everyone stop right where you are. This is the state police. We have you covered."

In thirty minutes the police had rounded up the Walls and all the men. They arrested and handcuffed them. Then everyone slowly walked down the dry creek bed to the valley where Jeanie and Rufus were.

The arrested people were put into police cars. Everyone went back to Sawdust.

Chapter 9

One Last Surprise

The next day Greg and Kirk went back to Peak's Valley to get their things. Rufus had stayed in Sawdust with Jeanie and her father.

When they got back to the gas station, Jeanie came running out. "We all have to go to the police station to see Officer Burns," she said. She got Rufus. Again, Kirk sat in the back of the pickup. Greg, Jeanie, and Rufus sat in front.

When they got to the police station, Officer Burns said, "Jeanie, what are you doing here? I just wanted to see *them*."

"Oh, I just wanted to see what was going on," she said.

Officer Burns said, "This is Mr. Downs from the bank here in town."

"Mr. Jennings," Mr. Downs said to Rufus, "we took a piece of rock from the police yesterday. We looked at it and tested it."

"That's my gold," Rufus said.

"That's not gold," Mr. Downs said. "It is a very high grade uranium ore. The hill is full of it. That is not The Three Aces mine. It is still up there somewhere."

At first Rufus looked sad. Then he looked happy. He didn't care about the uranium. He still wanted to find The Three Aces.

Then Officer Burns said, "The Wall gang has been wanted by the police for a long time. They made one very bad mistake when they tried to scare people away by using Bigfoot. That brought attention to the Valley. They might have gotten away with it except for that. When the newspapers started to write about Bigfoot, the Walls ended up having to hurt more people. Kirk, you and Greg will share a reward for helping catch them. We will send it to your home."

Jeanie said, "Well, you guys sure had some camping trip!"

"You're not kidding," Kirk said.

Then Officer Burns said, "There are some men here from the big newspapers. They want to talk to all of you."

In the next room were six men. They asked Greg, Kirk, Rufus, and Jeanie a lot of questions. They took pictures of them. One of the men said he would pay Kirk for the pictures of the Bigfoot costume. Finally Officer Burns said, "That's all. The boys have to head for home now."

"It's a long drive," Greg said.

"Rufus and I can walk back to the station," Jeanie said. "Dad will drive him to the Valley. Are you going to get some gas before you head back home?" she asked.

"We sure are," Greg said.

Jeanie left with Rufus.

Mr. Downs said, "You don't have to worry about Rufus. He already is a very, very rich man. He has found lots of gold for years. He has lots of money."

"Before you leave," Officer Burns said, "I think you'll want these." He gave Kirk the pictures of the Bigfoot costume and gave Greg his rifle that had been stolen by the Wall gang.

Greg and Kirk went out to the pickup.

"Can you beat that?" Kirk said. "This whole thing has been crazy."

"Well," Greg said, "you got your pictures. They weren't of Bigfoot. But they did help the police."

They drove back to Jeanie's station. They filled the tank. "This is on the house," Jeanie said. "Come back again."

"Yeah," said Rufus. "Don't wait too long. We'll look for the mine together. I think I'm going to live here in Sawdust for awhile. Come back soon."

Greg and Kirk took off. They headed back home. They would have a lot to tell their friends.

"They'll never believe us," said Greg.

"Oh, no?" smiled Kirk. "Then we'll just let them read about us in the newspapers!"